At the top of a very tall hill in a very small place called **Woollybottom**, is a horseshoe of houses.

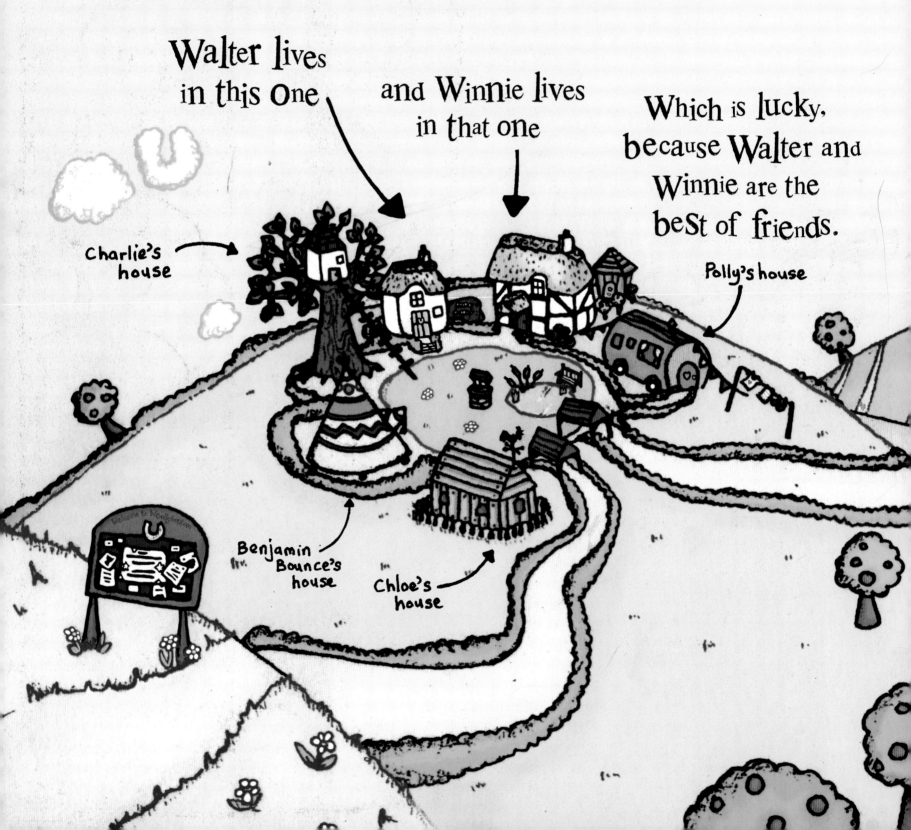

Walter lives in this one

and Winnie lives in that one

Which is lucky, because **Walter** and **Winnie** are the best of friends.

Charlie's house

Polly's house

Benjamin Bounce's house

Chloe's house

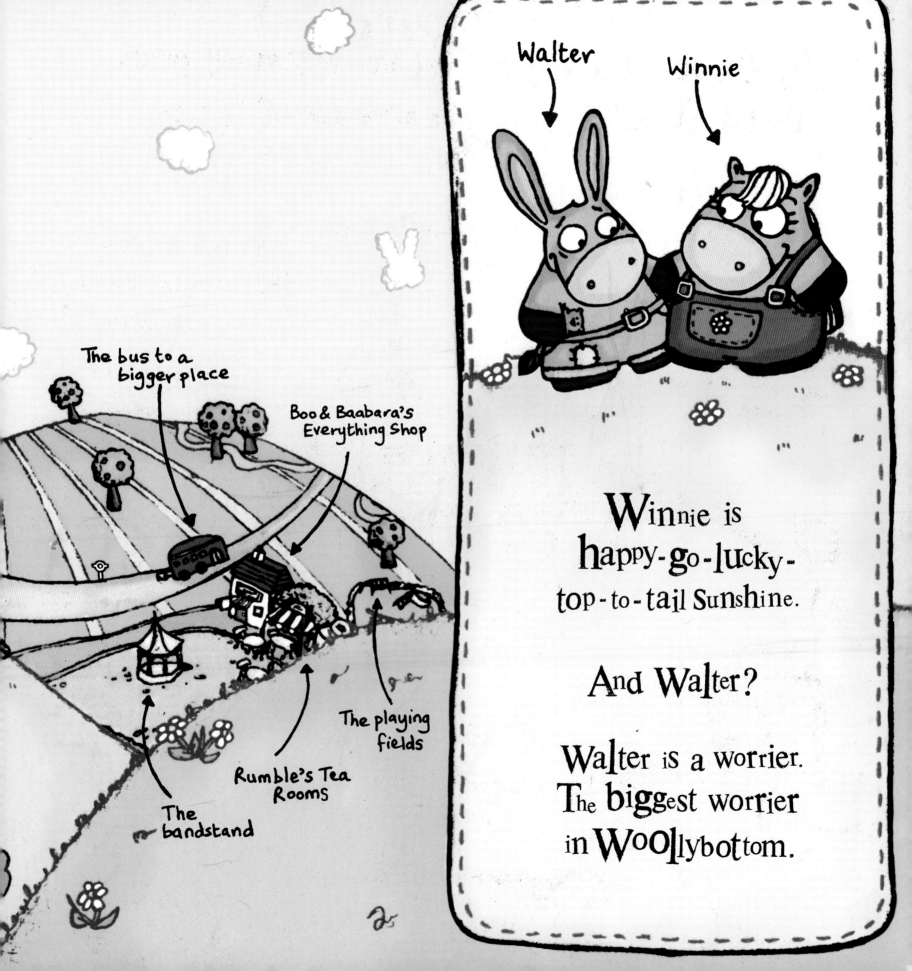

The bus to a bigger place

Boo & Baabara's Everything Shop

The playing fields

Rumble's Tea Rooms

The bandstand

Walter

Winnie

Winnie is happy-go-lucky-top-to-tail Sunshine.

And Walter?

Walter is a worrier. The biggest worrier in Woollybottom.

Usually, he worries about everyday things like...

the dream he had about a Chocolate-eating monster coming true.

Or...how terrible it would be if he lost Mr Teddy one day.

Sometimes he even worries that there is something he's forgotten to worry about.

But this story is about the time when Walter's worries got seriously BIG.
Yes, this story is about the week of...

You see, Walter did not particularly like Sport. It made him worry.
But guess what? He'd been picked for not ONE,
not two, but THREE events!

Oh my goodness... how this made him WOrry.

'I bounce SO HIGH and am winning SO MUCH
that my trousers Completely COME OFF...
and at that very moment, a TV CREW arrives
and films the no trousers thing, and so I am basically

on TV in just my PANTs!'

Chloe raised a
Cowbrow and Chuckled.
'Don't worry, Walter,
that won't happen.'

'It might,'
said Walter.

Just then, along came Polly.
'Hey, Walter, what's up?' she asked.

'Oh, Polly!'
said Walter.

'I've been picked for the
Champion Cheese-Eating
event on Sunday, but even though
Cheese is my **absolute favourite**,
I can't possibly do it, because

What if...

'A giant mouse ALSO enters, because he saw me on TV in just my PANTS. And what if I am SO good at eating cheese that I eat ALL the cheese in the WHOLE UNIVERSE and so he gets really angry and stamps on my HOUSE until it's FLAT!'

Polly and Chloe chuckled. 'Don't worry, Walter, that won't happen,' they said.

CHAMPION CHEESE-EATING

'It might',
said Walter.

Charlie and Benjamin Bounce arrived too.
'Hey, Walter, what's up?' they asked.

'Oh, Charlie! Oh, Benjamin!
I'm supposed to be doing the
Running Quite Fast event on Sunday,
but I can't possibly do it, because

What if...

'I run SO fast that I don't see the big hole made by the GIANT mouse who saw me on Tv. And so I fall down the hole and it goes THROUGH THE WHOLE WORLD and I tumble out into SPACE, where four ALIENS catch me...

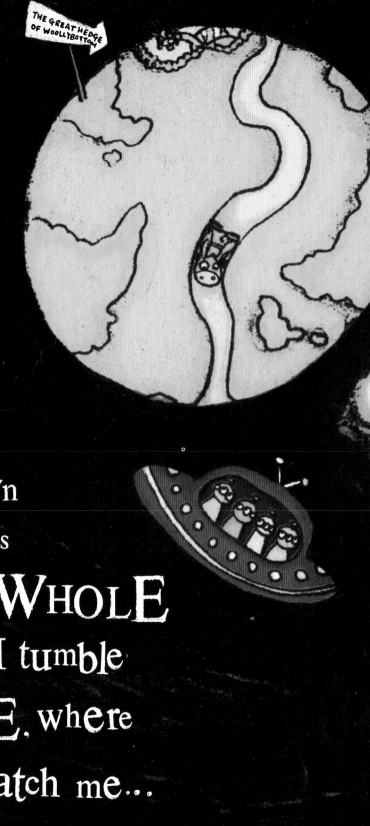

And what if I have to live on their planet forever which you'd think might be lucky because my house is flat, but the only food on the alien planet is bananas...

I HATE bananas!'

'Don't worry, Walter,' everyone chuckled.
'That won't happen!'

'It might,' said Walter.

Luckily, just when Walter thought he might POP with worry, his bestest friend Winnie arrived.

'What's up, Walter?' she smiled.

'Walter's worried about Sunday,' said Chloe.

'Walter's worried about EVERYTHING,' said Benjamin Bounce.

'No need to worry, Walter, leave it to us!' Winnie said.

Winnie always knew what to do.

And off they went.

In Winnie's Workshop the Woollybottomers got to work.

They sketched and stitched and glued and hammered and together they hatched a plan to solve Walter's worries.

They had made Walter his Very Own...

NO-NEED-TO-WORRY SUIT!

Walter couldn't believe his eyes.

He was so happy he decided to practise his events at home...

But when he tried bouncing, the non-banana snacks were so heavy, he was **Very** un-bouncy indeed.

Worse than that, he couldn't eat any cheese because of the anti-giant-mouse-stamping helmet.

And as for running quite fast...

Well, the magic stay-on trousers were rather tight, so he got himself in a bit of a pickle...

And whenever Walter was in a pickle, he called Winnie.

'Erm, hi, Winnie,' he said. 'I'm a little bit stuck about something. I love my new Suit, but, I sort of can't do anything properly when I have it On.'

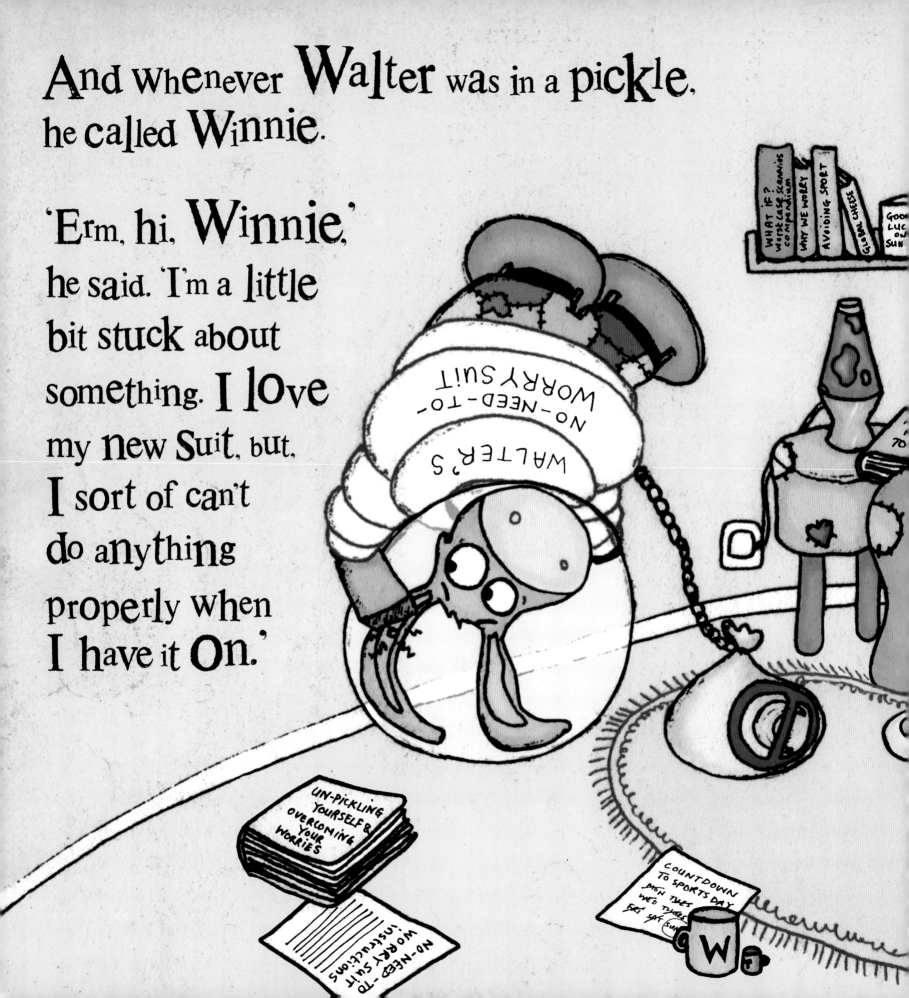

'No need to worry, Walter,' Winnie smiled.

'I know you'll figure out the best thing to do.'

But Walter was STILL worrying when sports day started, and all the way through his first event...

...which didn't go terribly well.

AND all the way through his SECOND event, which didn't go brilliantly either...

And Walter was STILL worrying when his very LAST race of the day was about to start...

'On your marks,' said the loudspeaker, 'Get Set...'

SUDDENLY, Walter knew EXACTLY what to do...

'GO!'

He flung off
his suit... and ran faster
than he'd ever run before!

You see, what this story is really about,
is the time when Walter realised that with
a little help from your friends...

...you can leave
your worries behind you.

THE WOOLLYBOTTOM

FREE

WEEKLY TRUMPET
NEWS FROM A LOVELY PLACE

WALTER WINS!!

'We always knew Walter could do it,' said Winnie, Walter's best friend and spokeshorse for the main Woollybottom crew.

NO-NEED-TO WORRY SUIT FOR SALE

AS NEW ☆ (NO LONGER NEEDED)

(SLIGHTLY NIBBLED NON-BANANA SNACKS)

MORE PHOTOS INSIDE......

& OTHER NEWS !

BOO BOUNCES HER WAY TO A NEW WOOLLYBOTTOM RECORD !

NATIONAL CHEESE SHORTAGES

UNDERCOVER MOLE

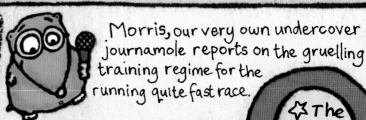

Morris, our very own undercover journamole reports on the gruelling training regime for the running quite fast race.

NEXT WEEK IN WOOLLYBOTTOM:

☆ The Grand Bi-Annual Banquet ☆

For all the Amazing people I am lucky enough to call my friends. With you in my life, I know for sure that I haven't a worry in the world.

& with special you-got-me-to-the-finish-line love to Robbie & Elvis & of course to Mandy, Helen & the whole HC crew.

First published in paperback in Great Britain by
HarperCollins Children's Books in 2012

1 3 5 7 9 10 8 6 4 2

ISBN: 978-0-00-744548-6

HarperCollins Children's Books is a division of HarperCollins Publishers Ltd.

Text and illustrations copyright © Rachel Bright 2012.

The author/illustrator asserts the moral right to be identified as the author/illustrator of this work.

Visit our website at: www.harpercollins.co.uk
Printed and bound in China